W9-DDR-811

Sunne is a magical being or "magbee." Nyame, the Creator of the planet Wiase, imbues Sunne with the power of the sun. Sunne's straight-haired siblings, Earthe, Watre, and Winde, have unique powers of their own.

When Sunne is teased and bullied by siblings because of Sunne's kinky and spirally afro-textured hair, Sunne desperately tries to change. Join Sunne and the other magbees, as they learn that there is beauty and power in difference. The message of self-love and bullying prevention in Sunne's Gift, coupled with its sci-fi imagery, make it a hit with people of all ages.

About the Author

Ama Karikari-Yawson,Esq. earned her BA from Harvard University, an MBA from the Wharton School, and a JD from the University of Pennsylvania Law School. Her unique understanding of social issues, business, and the law has enabled her to become a relevant voice and sought-after speaker on issues as varied as education, cultural sensitivity, bullying, sexual violence, and personal empowerment.

In 2013, a painful experience with bullying inspired her to write her best-selling fable about difference, *Sunne's Gift*. Ms. Karikari-Yawson became so personally invested in spreading the book's message of healing and harmony that she quit her six-figure job as a securities lawyer to become a full-time, author, storyteller, and educator.

Through her company, Milestales Publishing and Education Consulting, she publishes and distributes books and lesson plans. Additionally, she facilitates life-changing workshops and training sessions that incorporate storytelling, drama, dance, history, cutting edge psychological research, and legal analysis in order to truly propel participants towards healthier and more successful lives.

Her other books include the *Kwanzaa Nana Is Coming to Town* series, which introduces a folkloric character to the Kwanzaa holiday. She can be reached at milestalespublishing.gmail.com, and you can follow her work at https://www.facebook.com/milestales and www.milestales.com.

About the Illustrator

Rashad is a graduate of Tufts University, graduating with a BA in

Anthropology and a minor in Mandarin Chinese Language and Culture. His interests and passions are varied, ranging from the study of people and culture to performance art, fine art, and fiction writing.

He is also a self-taught freelance illustrator and aspiring animator, specializing in fantasy/sci-fi and cartoon illustration, using digital, pencil and pen mediums.

Mr. Malik Davis thoroughly enjoyed working on *Sunne's Gift* and is deeply committed to sharing its message of self-love, self-acceptance, and bullying prevention.

Please like Rashad's work on Facebook:
https://www.facebook.com/ramalikillustrations.

Dear Dr. Francis,
You are a stellar educator!
Commitment, dedication, and
innovation are several of
your qualities. Continue to
raise a new generation of
leaders. You give the world
new hope!

SUNNE'S GIFT

10/27/17

Sunne's Gift
By Ama Karikari Yawson

Copyright © 2016 by Ama Karikari Yawson
All rights reserved.

Graphic Design by Daisy Lew and Emil Rivera
Illustration by Rashad Malik Davis

All Rights Reserved. No part of this book may be used or reproduced by any mechanical, photographic or electronic process, or in the form of a phonographic recording; nor may it be stored in a retrieval system, transmitted, or otherwise be copied for public or private use without prior written permission of the publisher.

The intent of the author and publisher is to inspire each reader to love and respect his or her own God-given gifts and those of others. Although the author and publisher cannot assume responsibility for the awesome feats that each reader will achieve with this renewed love and respect, they wish that they could.

Published by Milestales: Stories That Help Us Go The Distance
www.milestales.com

Library of Congress Control Number: 2014901367
Second Edition

ISBN 978-0-9914808-1-4

_____ loves you

and purchased this spectacular book for you, _____,

because like Sunne, you are different. You are like no other person in the universe.

This book will help you to always remember that your unique qualities make you

both BEAUTIFUL and POWERFUL. Continue to revel in your own truth.

In the beginning, the planet Wiase was not as it is today.

There was no sun to provide warmth or light.
There was no earth from which fruit,
vegetables, or flowers could grow.
There was no water to quench the thirst of the living.
There was no wind to transport seeds or
provide a refreshing breeze.

The Creator, Nyame, had become bored with the barren planet Wiase. In an instant, and with just a thought, Nyame brought forth the sun, earth, water, and wind. Sunshine illuminated lush vegetation growing from the brilliant earth. The sounds of water flowing and breezes blowing produced a beautiful melody.

It was so good. But Nyame wanted to create more planets. "I'll make children to help me take care of this planet, Wiase." Nyame said. In an instant, and with just a thought, Nyame brought forth four magical beings or "magbees": Sunne, Earthe, Watre, and Winde.

Nyame addressed the magbees.

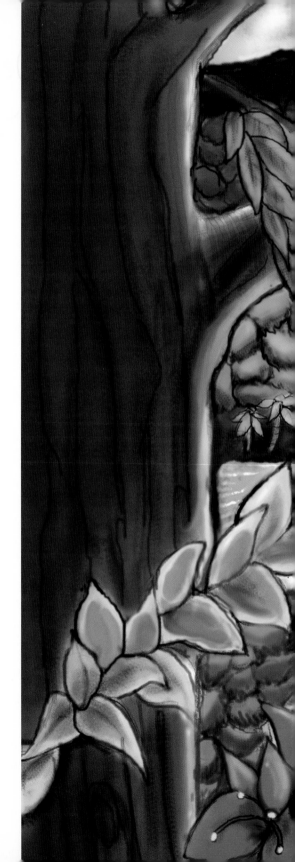

"Sunne, you are imbued with the power of the sun. For this reason, your skin is sun-darkened red, and your hair grows in spirally twists toward the sun. Take care of yourself, for the sun dwells within you."

"Earthe, you are imbued with the power of the earth. For this reason, your skin is brown, and your straight hair grows toward the soil. Take care of yourself, for the earth dwells within you."

"Watre, you are imbued with the power of water. For this reason, your skin is translucent green, and your straight hair flows down your back like water. Take care of yourself, for the waters dwell within you."

"Last, Winde, you are imbued with the power of the wind.
For this reason, your skin is gray, and your straight hair blows
with the breeze. Take care of yourself, for the wind dwells within you."

"You are all my children, made in my image. Love one another and treasure each other's gifts. Goodbye and I love you all." Nyame's voice faded, as Nyame went off to create other planets.

The four magbees were very responsible.

Sunne did a wave dance every morning and evening to make the sun rise and set.

By doing hip circles
every afternoon,
Earthe put nutrients
into the soil.

When the soil became dry, Watre did finger jiggles to summon the rain.

Winde blew out gaseous gusts of air that carried seeds to new places.

In their spare time, the magbees climbed trees
and played hide-and-seek. They also sang.
"Prim pra na na, prim pra na na, we are having so much fun!
Prim pra na na, prim pra na na, taking care of Wiase for everyone."

One day, the four magbees travelled to a river. They looked down at their reflections. For the first time, it occurred to them that Sunne looked different. Earthe, Winde, and Watre all had hair that lay flat and grew downward. But Sunne's hair stood tall.

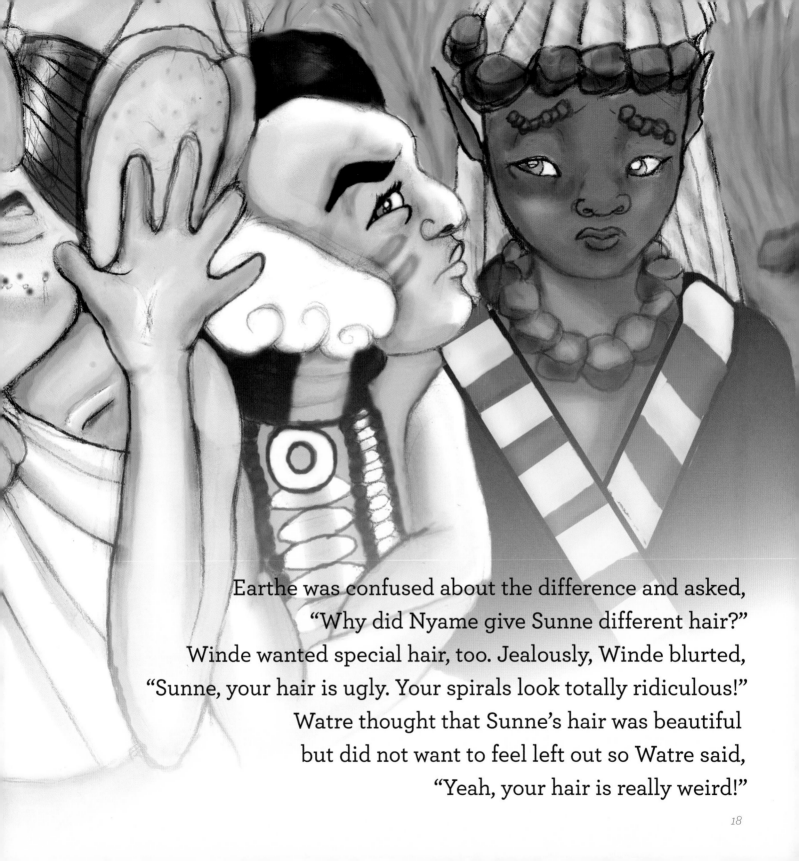

Earthe was confused about the difference and asked,
"Why did Nyame give Sunne different hair?"
Winde wanted special hair, too. Jealously, Winde blurted,
"Sunne, your hair is ugly. Your spirals look totally ridiculous!"
Watre thought that Sunne's hair was beautiful
but did not want to feel left out so Watre said,
"Yeah, your hair is really weird!"

Sunne's heart sank. Tears formed in Sunne's eyes.
Sunne did not want to be different, ugly, ridiculous, or weird.

Sunne picked up a stick and began to beat each spiral
of hair to make it straight. With each slap, Sunne's head
ached and Sunne felt weaker. But Sunne continued,
as Earthe, Winde, and Watre began to sing.

"You must! You must! It's worth the fuss!
Soon you will look like the rest of us!"

But when the last spiral of hair became straight, all of Sunne's hair fell out.

The sun disappeared, and darkness descended upon the land. Sunne, Earthe, Winde, and Watre looked around in horror!

Sunne did the wave dance again and again, but still there was no sun. Earthe, Watre, and Winde tried to do the wave dance, but still there was no sun. In a flash, the words of Nyame came to them.

"Sunne, you are imbued with the power of the sun. For this reason, your skin is sun-darkened red, and your hair grows in spirally twists toward the sun. Take care of yourself, for the sun dwells within you." By destroying Sunne's gift of spirally hair, they had destroyed Sunne's power of the sun.

The silver glow of the moon did not provide enough light for their games. The fruit trees, corn, and other vegetation began to die. The magbees felt weak with hunger.

In their collective grief, they chanted
"Nyame! Nyame! We are so sorry for what we have done.
We have destroyed our power of the sun!
Oh how, oh how can our mistake be undone?"
They waited for Nyame to answer. They could feel Nyame's presence,
but they did not hear Nyame's voice. The magbees sat and cried.

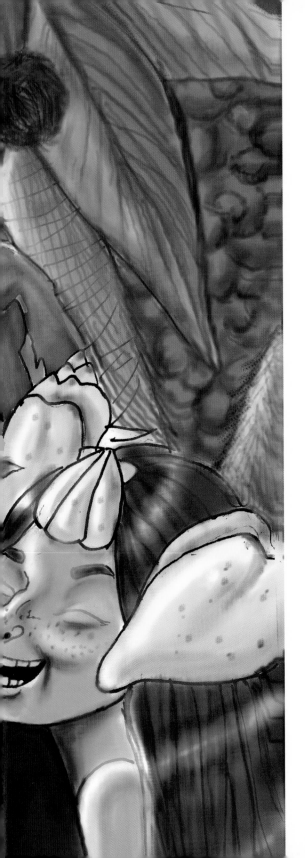

Finally Nyame said, "My children,
I forgive you all. I see that you have
learned your lesson. I made no mistakes
in creating you all with your beautiful
and varied colors, hair types, and
features. You all are equal in power but
distinct in your gifts. Never destroy
your own gift because you covet
someone else's. I love you all."
Nyame's voice faded.

At that moment, Sunne's spirally twists
grew back, and the sun reappeared.
Sunne felt alive and powerful again.
The magbees jumped up and down with
glee, thanking Nyame.

Then, the magbees
walked back to the
river and looked at
themselves again.

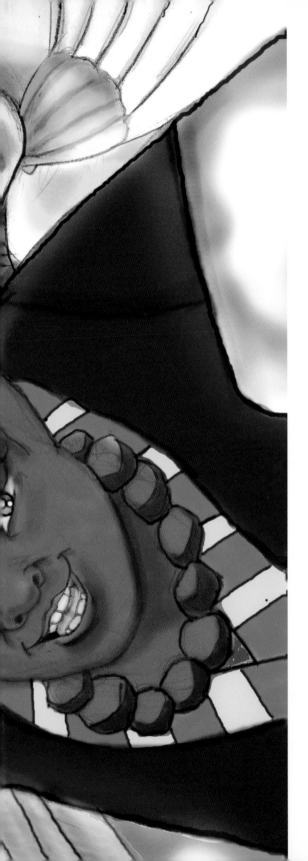

Sunne admired the beauty reflected. Sunne said, "I should not have destroyed my hair. My lovely spirals are what make me special and what makes me special makes me great. Earthe, Watre, and Winde agreed, and then all of the children sang.

"Sunne's beautiful: we can't deny!
In Sunne's hair, the sun's power lies.
We're all special in our own way.
We should celebrate each other
every day!"

CURRICULUM

READING COMPREHENSION

1 • Who is Nyame?

2 • What was Wiase like in the very beginning?

3 • Why did Nyame make the four magbees?

4 • Why did Nyame make each magbee look different?

5 • What did the magbees notice at the river?

6 • How did the magbees react to what they noticed?

7 • Why did Sunne want straight hair, and what did Sunne do to get it?

8 • What happened after Sunne's hair became straight?

9 • What did Earthe, Watre, Winde, and Sunne do to resolve the problem?

10 • Why did the children say, "We have destroyed our power of the sun"?

11 • What does it mean to be "equal in your power but distinct in your gifts"?

12 • What lessons did Earthe, Watre, Winde, and Sunne learn?

13 • This story focuses on Sunne's experience of bullying and self-mutilation. But what would have happened if the other magbees had experienced bullying and tried to destroy their hair, skin, or other features?

SCIENCE AND MATH

1 • What are the properties of water, soil, air, and the sun?

2 • Why did the vegetation begin to die when there was no sun?

3 • In *Sunne's Gift*, the magbees were sad when all of a sudden it switched from day to night. But nighttime is not a bad time. From a scientific perspective, why do we need darkness just as much as we need light?

4 • The story of *Sunne's Gift* provides a folkloric metaphor for a scientific process by which plants convert sunlight into the energy needed for their growth. Identify the name of that scientific process and describe it in greater detail.

5 • When the sun disappeared the four magbees entered a very challenging time in which resources were becoming scarce. Create and solve imaginative math problems pertaining to the amount of time before the resources would be exhausted. Example: There is only one surviving tree on Wiase. That tree has 24 oranges and each magbee eats 2 oranges per day. How long will it take for the magbees to finish the oranges, assuming that the oranges remain fresh?

6 • When Nyame answered the magbees calls for help and restored Sunne's hair, Wiase entered a state of immediate growth, abundance, and restoration. Create imaginative math problems pertaining to growth. Example: If there are 900 orange trees on the planet of Wiase and each of them grows 50 oranges in the 1 minute that it takes Nyame to restore the planet, how many oranges are available when the restoration is complete?

7 • The magbees take care of planet Wiase. How do you take care of planet Earth?

PSYCHO-SOCIAL STUDIES

1 • In the story, Nyame created the planet Wiase and the magbees with thoughts. What do you create with your thoughts?

2 • In the story, Nyame made the magbees different because they represented different forces of nature. Why do you think that human beings have different colors and features?

3 • In the story, Earthe, Watre, and Winde bullied Sunne by saying Sunne's hair is different, ugly, ridiculous, and weird. Go back to the text of the story. What were the three emotions or mental states that motivated Earthe, Watre, and Winde to be mean to Sunne?

4 • How should have Earthe, Watre, and Winde managed those three emotions or mental states? What should they have said to Sunne?

5 • Unfortunately, Earthe, Watre, and Winde did engage in bullying in the story. How do you think that Sunne should have reacted to Earthe, Watre, and Winde's bullying behavior?

6 • Have you ever been teased or teased other people? Please describe your own experience.

7 • Do you ever feel like changing yourself to fit in? Please describe your own experience.

8 • Sunne's special gift was the sun. What special gifts do you have?

9 • What would happen to the world if you did not share your gift?

CREATIVE ACTIVITIES

1 • Create your own illustrations of *Sunne's Gift*.

2 • Take some time to really think about the themes of *Sunne's Gift*, as well as the behaviors, movements, and voices of the four magbees. Now, write, direct, and perform a dramatic play based on *Sunne's Gift*.

3 • Using clay, playdoh, or paper mache, create your own model(s) of the the planet Wiase as described in *Sunne's Gift*.

4 • Write a poem or a song about your special gifts and talents.

5 • To someone you know, write a special letter expressing why you think that he or she is so wonderful and special.

To share your creative projects with the world go to https://www.facebook.com/milestales.
For the answer key, coloring pages, and Sunne Pledge, go to www.milestales.com.

Matthew Queenette and Michael Tim Aisha Yasmin Margaret Ama Delores Charles, Miles and Jojo Sam Amiko Kiratiana Yehoda Karyn Jman Andrea T. Rachel C. Erica S. Tamecca God's Finest Desiree L. Vivian Latoya Ishmael Emerson Nura and Salih Sheila Owen Yaw Nadira Emily Loretta Rupak and Nancy Anna and Matti Rachel B. AC Yuni and Miishe Marquetta Georgiana Kristy Antoinette Misee Frederick and Durwah Claudette Kourtney and Tim Eboni Tashanna Alana Christelyn Uche Adebola and Abiola Tamara Amma Frances Delilah Anima Michael T. Cameron Ingrid Catherine Michael K. Ashley Kendall Nedera Genevieve Mackenzi Denaka Gloria T. Linda Sarika Charles Nadeen Helen and Kevin Rita Barbara, Gerald, Gerry and Grace Patricia D. Alicia Aunty Awurama Jeffrey B. Joe Weslee Kathryn Arthur Collins Charing Lauren Fonny Phoebe Mindy Daphnie and Steve Max Muriel Casey Najah Bianca and Rob Brandon Kimberly Ivory Mary G. Chelsea & Claudia Andrea D. Deandra Kim Samantha Priya and Samit Shalari Sharifa Rachel P. Vanessa H. John Claudia and Ethan Christina Lacey Laura Nicholas Jackie Khadhyja Nancy Vanessa B. Katie Sheryl Mary P. Narcisa Deuel Steven Autumn Nicole and Monique Caron Angela Ursula Holly Kate & Ryan Cindy Vedra Rafa Nana Akua Belinda Hoai Moina and Amol Patricia H. Enoch Mosi Dave A. Barbara Alberta Regina Aziza Maureen Toby Carmen D. Gloria A. Ian Leah Zahiyya Luke Lea Salima Zakiyyah Bernice Nnenna Carmen C. Eyana Godfred Judith Jeneba Desiree D. Natasha Johanna Monica Erica W. Elana Darin David B. Abeni Shira Nathaniel Victor Tiffany Mynaturalreality Eugene Shayla Louis Missy Edgewood School Kojo and Paulina Carleeta Julien Rachel N. Ji Heather Debra Marvin Brenda Katherine Patience Sarah Linnea Kia Bill Indira Blue Lurie Supriya Samara Yoshiko Ayele Kate Dave N. Jeffrey P. Alisha Elwin

Thank You